COREY'S TERRIBLE RIDE

Sam wouldn't slow down, and he wouldn't get back in line. He was totally out of control. There was only one thing for Corey to do. That was to get him to gallop right back into the stable.

For once Sam did what Corey said. He galloped right past the gate and into the stable and didn't stop until he got to his stall.

Corey could hear the music and the clop of horse and pony hooves out in the ring. She could hear the audience clapping for the performers. The drill demonstration was going on without her!

Somehow Corey managed to dismount and put Sam in the stall. She loosened his girth, then slammed the door and locked it.

"I'm so mad at Sam!" Corey sobbed. "I'm never riding again!"

Corey
in the Saddle

BONNIE BRYANT

Illustrated by Marcy Ramsey

A SKYLARK BOOK
NEW YORK • TORONTO • LONDON • SYDNEY • AUCKLAND

RL 3, 007–010
COREY IN THE SADDLE
A Skylark Book / March 1996

*Skylark Books is a registered trademark of Bantam Books,
a division of Bantam Doubleday Dell Publishing Group, Inc.
Registered in U.S. Patent and Trademark Office and elsewhere.
Pony Tails is a trademark of Bonnie Bryant Hiller.*

*"USPC" and "Pony Club" are registered trademarks of The United
States Pony Clubs, Inc., at The Kentucky Horse Park, 4071 Iron Works
Pike, Lexington, KY 40511-8462.*

ISBN 0-553-48378-1

Published simultaneously in the United States and Canada

*Bantam Books are published by Bantam Books, a division of Bantam
Doubleday Dell Publishing Group, Inc. Its trademark, consisting of the
words "Bantam Books" and the portrayal of a rooster, is Registered in U.S.
Patent and Trademark Office and in other countries. Marca Registrada.
Bantam Books, 1540 Broadway, New York, New York 10036.*

PRINTED IN THE UNITED STATES OF AMERICA

OPM   0 9 8 7 6 5 4 3 2 1

Corey
in the Saddle

1 Just for the Animals

"Oh, how cute!" Corey Takamura cooed. She was looking at a sleeping kitten, curled up into a tiny ball. He clutched a rubber mouse toy in his paws. "Look at him, you guys," she told her two best friends.

Jasmine James gazed at the kitten. "Aww," she said, agreeing with Corey.

"He's adorable," May Grover said. "Check out the puppies."

Corey and Jasmine looked where May was pointing. Two puppies were roughhousing, rolling around in the newspaper strips in their cage.

"All the animals are cute," Jasmine said with a sigh.

A smile crept across Corey's face. May and Jasmine didn't know it, but her plan was working.

Pony Tails

In a few minutes the three girls would be riding their ponies in a demonstration for a huge audience. Their Pony Club, Horse Wise, was trying to raise money for CARL—the County Animal Rescue League.

The girls had been getting ready for the demonstration for a long time. May and Jasmine were very nervous about riding in front of a big crowd. So Corey had decided to show them the animals from CARL. Sure enough, once May and Jasmine saw the pets in the trailer that CARL had set up at Pine Hollow Stables for the day, they forgot all about being nervous.

May crouched down to look at a baby raccoon in a cage. "Can someone adopt this raccoon, too?" she asked Corey.

Corey shook her head. "No. He's a wild animal. CARL was just taking care of him for a while. I think most of the other animals here can be adopted today, though."

May stared at the raccoon through the bars of the cage. He stared back at her. She made a funny face at him. He stared back at her.

"No sense of humor," she commented.

"Maybe you just don't know how to tell a joke in raccoon," Jasmine said. May giggled. The raccoon scooted back in his cage, away from May.

Corey in the Saddle

"I'm not going to hurt you," she said.

"It's good for him to be scared of you," Corey reminded her. "He's going to be released back into the wild soon."

May thought about that. It made sense. Animals who were going to live in the wild *should* be afraid of humans. That way they'd be more independent and safe.

Corey knew a lot about animals. Her mother was a veterinarian whom everyone called Doc Tock. Doc Tock had her own practice, but she also did a lot of work at CARL. May thought it was fun living next door to a vet—especially since May, Jasmine, and Corey were all crazy about animals. The girls were really crazy about ponies. That was why they called themselves the Pony Tails.

"*Bleeaaaaaa!*"

A sudden noise startled the girls.

"What was that?" Jasmine said. They looked around to see where it had come from.

There was a cage in the corner behind the other cages. It had a lot of newspaper torn up in it. Corey peered at the cage—she couldn't see an animal in there.

"*Bleeaaaaa!*"

The sound was definitely coming from the cage in the corner. Slowly the girls went over to investigate.

Pony Tails

The Pony Tails stared at the pile of shredded newsprint. Corey watched in surprise as the paper rustled. Then a tiny black nose popped out from under the papers. It sniffed curiously. Then came a furry mouth. The tiny mouth opened and made a great big noise.

"Bleeaaaaa!"

"It's a goat!" Corey declared. "A baby goat!"

The goat had black-and-white splotched hair and bright black eyes.

The Pony Tails watched as the small creature tried to stand up. First its little rear legs pushed upward. Then its spindly front legs began working.

"It's so cute," breathed Jasmine. "I bet it's only a few weeks old."

Corey nodded. The creature *was* tiny. She knew from her mother that CARL rescued and took in all kinds of animals. What had happened to this tiny goat? she wondered. He was definitely too young to be separated from his mother. Maybe he'd been orphaned.

Corey looked at the papers hanging from the goat's cage. She was right. According to his chart, his mother had died.

"Poor little guy," May said as she read the information. "He seems to like our company, though, doesn't he?"

The goat was bleating softly. He ambled over

to the front of the cage to get a better look at the girls.

Corey's heart melted as she looked into his dark eyes. The goat bleated again. The soft, sad sound reminded Corey that it was important to help sick and abandoned animals. She was glad that that was what their Pony Club was doing today.

"There you are, girls!" Mrs. Reg said as she burst into the trailer. "Come on, you three—it's almost time to mount up!"

"We're coming," May told the older woman. "We're just talking to the animals."

Mrs. Regnery was the stable manager at Pine Hollow. That was the stable where the Pony Tails took riding lessons and had Pony Club meetings. Everybody called her Mrs. Reg.

The girls said good-bye to the tiny goat and the other animals. "We have to tack up our ponies now," Jasmine told them.

As the girls followed Mrs. Reg back to the stable, Corey looked up at the people in the stands. What a huge crowd, she thought. All these people had come to see the drill demonstration!

"Thanks for bringing us to the CARL trailer, Corey," Jasmine said. "After seeing those animals, I can't wait to ride."

"Me either," added May.

Corey in the Saddle

"Hurry up, girls," Mrs. Reg urged them again. "Thirty minutes till showtime."

"The Pony Tails will be ready," May promised.

The three girls separated and raced for their ponies' stalls.

As Corey turned the corner near Samurai's stall, her heart was thumping. She'd never seen such a big audience at Pine Hollow.

Jasmine and May were much calmer now.

But Corey was a nervous wreck!

2 The Drill Demonstration

The Pony Tails' ponies were very different from one another—just like their three owners. May's pony, Macaroni, was sweet and well-behaved. Outlaw, Jasmine's pony, could be mischievous and stubborn. Corey had gotten Samurai last year, right before her parents' divorce. Having Sam had helped Corey a lot then, and she still loved to ride and train her pony.

Corey's mother said training a pony was a long, hard job that required patience. So far, Corey thought, that was certainly true. Sam was a wonderful pony, but he also had an independent streak and sometimes liked to cause trouble.

As Corey approached his stall, Sam greeted her with a loud nicker. "Hi, boy," she said. She stroked the white blaze on his nose. It was crescent-shaped, like a samurai sword, which was how Sam had gotten his name.

Moving slowly, Corey began tacking him up. Sam hated this part of riding. Corey always tried to make it easier on him. She placed the saddle on his back and spoke softly. As she talked, Corey could feel butterflies fluttering in her stomach.

"You have to be good today, Sam," she said. Corey pictured the tiny goat and all the other animals in the trailer. They all needed the Pony Club's help. "The CARL animals are depending on us, you know. So is everyone in Horse Wise."

Sam didn't seem to care. As Corey put on his tack, he blew air out through his nose. He tossed his head impatiently.

"Calm down, boy," she said. She was starting to get worried.

Sam's *not* going to act up today, she told herself. There are too many people out there watching. He wouldn't dare ruin the show.

Today's demonstration was a drill. That meant that the riders and horses marched in formation. It also meant that even a tiny mistake would be noticed. That was especially true of the small drill demonstration. Max had chosen six riders to do a special performance. Corey was one of those riders.

Corey knew the worst thing to do was let Sam know she was nervous. Horses and ponies are very sensitive. Sam would sense her feelings and become nervous himself.

Corey tightened his girth and began to go over the movements of the drill in her head.

"Stay still, Sam!" Corey commanded as her restless pony kept moving around in his stall.

First we march out two by two, she thought. And then we . . .

Then we what? Suddenly Corey's mind went blank. What came next? Two by two, and then what?

Nearby, May was tacking up Macaroni. As usual the shaggy yellow pony stood patiently while his rider prepared him. Macaroni wasn't like Samurai, who was now pawing the ground.

"May?" Corey called out in a shaky voice. "What's our first move?"

May grinned at her. "Corey! Are you still testing me?" she asked. "Don't worry, I'm not nervous anymore. Like we told you, seeing the animals from CARL really helped. Now I just want to go out there and do the best job I can."

Corey turned to Jasmine. Her friend was adjusting Outlaw's stirrups. "Do you remember our first move after we enter the ring?" she asked.

"Did you really think I'd forget the big circle?" Jasmine called back. "That's my favorite part of the demonstration."

Corey sighed. Of course, their first move was the big circle. She'd done it hundreds of times. And then came the figure eights, and then . . .

Sam just wouldn't stay still. As Corey turned back to him, anger surged through her. She was having enough trouble remembering the drill. The last thing she needed just then was a stubborn, naughty pony.

"Calm down right now!" Corey snapped at her pony. "This is no time for you to be difficult!"

May looked at her in surprise. She'd never heard Corey speak so sharply to Sam.

The pony blinked at Corey. Then, to Corey's amazement, he stood patiently.

When she was finally done tacking him up, she carefully checked everything over. Her pony looked perfect. Now all Corey had to do was get his behavior to match his appearance.

"Riders, line up at the door!" Max Regnery called out. Max was Mrs. Reg's son and the owner and riding instructor at Pine Hollow. Right now he was rushing around, barking commands at all the riders.

"Corey! Sam!" he yelled. "Come on. We've got a full house out there. Line up in formation at the door."

"Okay," Corey replied. "Come on, Sam." She tugged gently at Sam's reins. He took one step forward and then stopped. She tugged again. This time the stubborn pony stood still. She tugged harder. Finally he got the message and followed her out of his stall.

As she led Sam to the door, Corey looked over at her friends. May was hugging Macaroni. Jasmine was giving Outlaw one final brushing. The two of them—and their ponies—looked perfectly calm.

But Corey's stomach was doing somersaults. Her throat was dry and tight. Her legs felt like rubber.

"Butterflies, Corey?" Lisa Atwood, an older rider, gave Corey a sympathetic smile.

Corey nodded numbly.

"A few butterflies are good," Lisa said. "They keep you on your toes. Just try not to let Sam know how nervous you are."

"It's too late," Corey said glumly. "He knows already, and he's making the most of it."

Lisa patted Corey's shoulder. "I'm sure you'll do fine. And you know what?" Lisa shrugged. "If you don't do fine, it's not the end of the world. Trust me, my friends and I have had some pretty bad shows."

Corey was still a little new to Pine Hollow, and she didn't know Lisa very well. But what she did know of her, she liked a lot. Lisa and her friends, Stevie Lake and Carole Hanson, were members of a group the three of them had started called The Saddle Club. They were horse-crazy, just like the Pony Tails were pony-crazy.

Corey tried to listen to Lisa's advice. "Thanks, Lisa." Corey managed a smile and continued on toward the door, where the riders were slowly gathering.

"Is my necktie straight?" one girl asked.

"Here, let me brush that dust off your breeches," said Jackie Rogers.

"If this horse tries to trot when I want him to walk, I think I'll . . . ," said Erin Mosley.

"I can't get this strap snapped." Amie Connor was having trouble with her hard hat.

"Time to mount up!" Max reminded the riders.

Corey climbed into Sam's saddle. Then, one by one, she and all the other riders touched the stable's good-luck horseshoe before falling into formation.

Touching the horseshoe was one of Pine Hollow's traditions. Nobody who touched the horseshoe before a ride had ever been seriously hurt in a riding accident. This time Corey didn't just touch the horseshoe. She rubbed it!

"Come on, my turn," said Erin, edging her pony between Corey and the wall.

May turned around and rolled her eyes. Corey giggled. For a minute she forgot about being nervous. Erin Mosley was not exactly the nicest member of their Pony Club. In fact, sometimes she was so nasty, it was kind of funny.

"Everybody smile," called out Mrs. Reg. Corey snapped back to attention as Max's mother checked over the riders one last time. "Riders, proceed," she said.

Corey swallowed hard as she filed into the arena behind the others. The sound of applause filled her ears.

"Wow!" Jasmine whispered. "Max said there are eight hundred and fourteen people watching. Now I believe it!"

Corey gulped. "Did you hear that, Sam? Eight hundred and fourteen! No funny business," she said.

As the music started, Corey gripped Sam's reins tightly. The pony tried to shake free. Corey tugged harder. This time the pony managed to yank the reins away from her. Corey nearly lost her balance trying to pull them back.

"Sam!" she hissed.

He twitched his ears in reply. Before Corey could do or say anything more, the ponies and their riders began to form the circle that was their second move.

But Sam had a different idea. His idea was to ignore Corey's signals. No matter what she told him to do—with her hands, her feet, her legs, or her whole body—Sam ignored it. Instead he did exactly what Quarter, the pony in front of him, did.

In the figure eight, Sam was supposed to go between Outlaw and Nero. But he dashed after Quarter and messed up the figure eight for all the other riders. When Quarter turned right at a trot, Sam was supposed to go left. He went right. That messed up the trotting segment.

Every time Sam did something wrong, Corey clutched more tightly at his reins. Soon she was holding the reins so tightly, her hands hurt! Sam didn't seem to notice. He just kept following Quarter.

"What's the matter?" May whispered as they walked two by two.

"Everything!" Corey said, trying to hold back tears. "I don't know how I'm going to get him to do the small drill exercise."

May nodded. Things did look terrible. The harder Corey tried to control Sam, the more he misbehaved.

The music got louder. It was near the end of the first demonstration and time for the riders to canter.

The second Quarter started cantering, Sam cantered, too. He cantered faster than the other pony. He caught up to him, and then he passed him. He wasn't supposed to do that!

"Sam!" This time Corey yelled at him. He brought his head down, and then he began to gallop around the ring!

He wouldn't slow down, and he wouldn't get back in line. He was totally out of control. There was only one thing for Corey to do: get him to gallop right back into the stable.

With the reins Corey told him which way to go. For once Sam did what she said. He galloped right past the gate and into the stable and didn't stop until he got to the door of his stall.

Corey could hear the music and the clop of the horse and pony hooves out in the ring. She could hear the audience clapping for the performers. The drill demonstration was going on without her!

Corey couldn't hold in the tears for one more second. They came and they kept on coming.

Somehow she managed to dismount and put Sam in the stall. She loosened his girth, then slammed the door and locked it. She was so angry, she didn't care about untacking her pony and cooling him down. Right now she wouldn't care if she never saw him again!

"Try not to take it so hard," a voice suddenly said.

Corey turned around. It was Red O'Malley, the head stablehand at Pine Hollow.

"It was only a demonstration," Red went on. "You and Sam had a bad day, but there will be plenty of other days. Besides, the crowd loves the show."

As tears streamed down her cheeks, Corey shook her head. She knew Red was trying to make her feel better, but it wouldn't work. Today was the most miserable day of her life. Thanks to her and Sam, the fund-raiser for CARL was ruined.

"I'm so mad at Sam," she said. "I'm never riding again." She let out a sob, then stumbled out of the stable. All she could think about was her awful performance. Why had Max bothered to choose her for the special drill? She was a terrible rider and now everyone knew it.

Without even looking where she was going, Corey wandered into one of Pine Hollow's empty paddocks.

Corey in the Saddle

Suddenly a familiar sound startled her.
"Bleeaaaaa!"
It was the baby goat.
What was he doing in his cage in the middle of the paddock?

3 Where Is Corey?

May could barely keep her mind on the drill demonstration. She and Macaroni performed well, but she wasn't even thinking about that. Instead she was thinking about Corey.

Jasmine was just as worried about their friend. She'd seen Corey and Sam gallop out of the ring. Sam had been misbehaving during the whole demonstration.

Poor Corey! Jasmine thought. Corey was usually the calm and steady one in their group. Jasmine had never seen her so upset.

Outlaw suddenly shook his head hard. Whoops! Jasmine thought. She'd been so worried about Corey, she'd forgotten to slow down. Luckily Outlaw had remembered.

Jasmine drew on the reins and sat into her saddle. Outlaw returned to a walk.

Corey in the Saddle

"Good boy," she whispered, and she patted his neck to thank him. It was bad enough that one rider had had to leave the ring. Jasmine didn't want to be the second!

Somehow Jasmine and May got through the demonstration. When it was over, the riders all lined up in the middle of the ring facing the audience. The music stopped, and the audience stood and clapped and cheered for them. Jasmine gave a smile and a little nod to her parents. May waved to her sisters. The audience cheered more loudly. May and Jasmine could see Doc Tock and Mr. Takamura in the stands. Both were clapping, but both also had worried expressions on their faces. Where was Corey?

Max walked proudly into the ring and took a bow. Then he turned to his riders and gave them the signal to file out of the ring. The first part of the demonstration was over. After a short break, the six riders would do the special drill. Jasmine wondered if Corey and Sam would be able to perform.

The riders trotted their horses and ponies out of the ring and into the stable. In May's ears, she could still hear the crowd clapping for them. But in her head, all she could hear were the words, "Where's Corey?" She looked at Jasmine. She didn't have to ask. Jasmine was wondering the same thing.

They could see that Sam was in his stall. His girth had been loosened and he was munching on hay. He didn't look ready to perform in the special drill, and there was no sign of Corey.

The girls put their ponies in their stalls, then met at Sam's stall. Max was there, too. He was looking at Sam.

"What about the small group demonstration?" May asked. "We've got to tell Corey it's time!"

Max shook his head. "I don't think Sam here is in any mood to perform for anybody."

"I bet Corey isn't, either," said Jasmine.

"I think you're right about that," Max agreed. "The rest of the riders will go ahead without her."

May and Jasmine exchanged miserable glances. After all her hard work, all those weeks of training, Corey would miss the special drill? This was terrible.

Max shrugged. "These things happen, girls. Everybody who works with horses knows that there are days when the horses just don't work. Or sometimes it's the riders. Right now what Corey needs most is a couple of friends. Do you know of any?"

May and Jasmine looked at one another.

Corey in the Saddle

"I think we know just the girls for the job," said Jasmine.

Max smiled. "See you later." He left to get the other five riders ready for the small group demonstration.

All around them in the stable, riders were busy and horses were excited. There was a lot of work to do in a short time.

The five riders who were going to proceed with the special demonstration were especially busy. They had to figure out how to do their performance without Corey.

"I don't think I can watch this, anyway," said May. "Not without Corey."

"I know what you mean," said Jasmine. "Let's find her."

They looked everywhere they could think of. They checked the loft. Corey wasn't there. They looked in the tack room. She wasn't there, either. They searched the feed room, even opening all the grain barrels. There was no sign of Corey.

Jasmine went out to the hay shed. May looked in the gardening shack. Together they checked Max's office and the locker area. Corey wasn't in any of those places.

They could hear the music of the demonstration. And when it was over, they heard the audience clapping. Then they heard a voice on the public address system. It was Judy Barker, the veterinarian who took care of the horses and ponies at Pine Hollow.

Judy thanked everybody who had come, then thanked everybody who had made a donation to CARL. She told them that they'd made a lot of money that afternoon. There was more applause.

"Hooray," Jasmine cheered softly. May made a thumbs-up sign. Both of the girls were happy that they'd helped the animals of CARL. But both of them were also sorry about Corey's ride. Maybe the news about the money would help cheer her up. The girls decided they *had* to find her.

"Maybe she went home," Jasmine suggested.

"Maybe," May agreed. "She's supposed to go to her father's tonight. Maybe she found him and they went to his apartment."

Since her parents had divorced, Corey spent half her time at her mother's house, which was between May's and Jasmine's homes. The other half she spent at her father's apartment, which was near Pine Hollow and school.

"I don't think so, May," Jasmine said suddenly. "There's her father now."

Mr. Takamura was hurrying into the stable. "Where's Corey?" he asked.

Corey in the Saddle

"We don't know," May said. "We thought maybe she was with you."

Then Corey's mother arrived at Sam's stall. "Have you seen her?" she asked May and Jasmine.

May shook her head. "We've looked everywhere."

"She was so excited about being chosen for the special demonstration," said Mr. Takamura. "It's a shame that Sam acted up."

"Maybe Corey got *too* excited," said Doc Tock. "Sam is very sensitive—he could have felt the pressure."

"Corey did seem a little nervous," said Jasmine thoughtfully. "She really wanted to help the animals from CARL."

May nodded. "She helped calm *us* down. But she made herself more nervous!"

Doc Tock looked worried. "I think we'd better find her," she said. "Could you girls take care of getting Sam home?"

"Sure," said May.

"Of course," Jasmine echoed. That had been the plan from the beginning. May's father would bring Sam home in his horse trailer, along with Macaroni and Outlaw.

May and Jasmine got right to work. First they took off Sam's tack. He still seemed highstrung and nervous. But when they began to groom him, the pony relaxed. The more they brushed and rubbed, the calmer he became.

"It's almost as if we're brushing the anger and tension out of him," said May.

"He really was tense, wasn't he?" said Jasmine.

"Sure was. And that made Corey nervous," May said.

"Or maybe, as Doc Tock said, it was the other way around," Jasmine suggested.

"Are you girls grooming Sam for Corey?" Red O'Malley asked.

"Yes," May told the stablehand. "Corey . . . uh . . ." Her words trailed off. She wasn't quite sure how to explain it.

"It's a shame about Sam," Red said with a shrug. "Just wasn't his day. I tried to tell Corey not to take it so hard."

"You saw her?" Jasmine asked. "Where was she?"

"I saw her after she put Sam in his stall," Red explained. "Like I said, I tried to tell her not to take it so hard. The poor kid was crying too much to listen. She mumbled something about never riding again. Then she wandered out of here, as if all she could think about was getting away from that pony of hers."

"Did you see where she went?" May asked.

Corey in the Saddle

Red shook his head. "No. After she left I went back to my favorite chore." He grinned. "Mucking out stalls."

"Thanks, Red," Jasmine said. "We'll see you later."

The two girls groomed Sam in silence for a few minutes.

Finally Jasmine spoke. "Did you hear that, May? Corey told Red she never wanted to ride again."

May nodded solemnly. "It's terrible. We can't let her do that. How can one of the Pony Tails give up riding?"

"But what can we do?" Jasmine asked. "We can't *make* her get on Sam again."

"You're right," May said slowly. A second later her face lit up. "I've got an idea."

"Uh-oh." Jasmine put her hands on her hips and stared at her friend. "Is this one of your little ideas, or a big one?" she demanded.

"A big one," May went on, sounding more and more excited. "Remember the first time Macaroni threw me?" she asked.

Jasmine nodded. "What does that have to do with anything?"

"A lot," May replied. "After that I felt just like Corey feels now. I was so mad at my pony, I didn't want to be with him. I even told my father I never wanted to ride again."

"But you got back into the saddle," Jasmine pointed out.

"That's right," May declared. "And that's because my father didn't force me."

"Huh?" Jasmine was confused. "Your father's a horse trainer. I thought riding instructors always made you get right back on the horse."

"Dad thinks it's best to let the rider decide that," May replied. "That's what we have to do with Corey," she said firmly. "Let her decide."

Jasmine stared at her friend. May's father knew a lot about horses. If he said the best thing to do was to leave it up to the rider, then that was what they should do.

The problem was, Jasmine knew a lot about May. And one thing she knew about May was that her big ideas sometimes went haywire. Corey was very important to the Pony Tails. They couldn't afford to make a mistake where she was involved.

"Are you sure about this, May?" Jasmine asked. "We shouldn't talk to Corey about Sam or the drill?"

"That's right," May said as she swept the brush over Sam's flank. "The best thing we can do is not say a word about ponies to Corey."

"But if we can't talk to her about ponies,

what are we going to talk about?" Jasmine asked.

"We'll think of something," May answered cheerfully.

Jasmine wasn't so sure. The Pony Tails not talking about ponies was like . . . grooming a pony without a curry comb. Impossible!

As she began combing out Sam's mane, Jasmine decided to go along with May's idea. But one more worry was nagging at her.

"Has your father tried this with lots of riders?" she asked May.

"Yup," May replied.

"What does he do if the rider won't get back on the horse?" Jasmine went on. "What if she *never* rides again?"

"Listen, Jasmine," May replied. "Corey's pony-crazy, just like us. She can't give up riding forever. We have to be patient, that's all."

Jasmine finished her part of grooming Sam, then dropped the tools into Corey's grooming bucket. She hoped May was right. But Red's words were still playing inside her head:

Corey mumbled something about never riding again.

4 Corey's New Friend

The goat lifted his head to look at Corey. She couldn't figure out what he was doing in his cage in the middle of the paddock.

She wiped the tears off her cheek. "What's the matter, little goat?"

As if to answer, the tiny kid nuzzled something in the torn newspaper that lined the bottom of his cage. Corey watched as he bit firmly at something, then lifted his head. It was his bottle. It was full of milk, but he couldn't get any of it. The bottle was supposed to be propped in a special holder. He'd obviously been so hungry, he'd pulled it out of the holder. Now he couldn't get a drop of milk out of it.

"I can help you," Corey said. She'd been useless with Sam, but she knew how to help the goat.

Corey in the Saddle

The goat blinked at her curiously. In spite of her tears, she smiled back. The little goat was very cute.

Corey had helped her mother take care of many orphaned animals like this one. All she had to do was clip the bottle back into the rack.

She opened the cage and reached in for the bottle. The kid nuzzled her hand.

She patted him softly and then scratched his neck. After a few seconds, he moved his head so that she could scratch the other side of his neck.

"Oh, so you're the boss now?" she teased him. She could have sworn he nodded.

Then he stepped back and leaned down toward the bottle. His message was clear.

Corey picked up the bottle. She was about to snap it back into the rack when the kid stuck his head out of the cage. He wanted *her* to feed him!

Corey helped the baby into her lap. Then she laid him down on his back in her crossed legs, his head resting on her left knee. She held the bottle in her right hand and offered it to him. He reached up eagerly, grabbing the nipple between his lips and sucking hard. Some of the milk dribbled out of his mouth and onto Corey's riding pants. Corey didn't mind. Most of it was getting where it belonged. That was the important part.

In a few minutes, the kid released the nipple. His little eyes shut and, before Corey knew what was happening, he fell sound asleep—right there in her lap!

She looked at his face. She saw nothing but trust and joy. She'd done everything right with this goat—how different it felt from being with Sam today!

Corey sighed. She loved Samurai—she really did. But sometimes he could be so stubborn and naughty.

Once not too long before, Sam had run away for a whole week. Then for five days last month, he'd refused to jump when everyone else in Pony Club was practicing jumping. And today he'd ruined the drill for everyone—the audience, the Pony Club, and Max. Corey wondered how Max had handled the special drill. It was supposed to be done with six riders, not five!

As she thought about today's performance, Corey got furious all over again. Then she remembered what her mother said: Training ponies was a long, hard job that required patience.

Well, I'm totally out of patience! Corey thought. Sam's on his own now!

Corey in the Saddle

In her lap, the goat stirred. Corey patted him gently, then glanced back over at his cage. This time Corey noticed the big red letters stamped across his paperwork. ADOPTED, they said.

That's good news, Corey thought. It meant he'd have a loving home.

But inside Corey felt a prickle of worry. Why had someone just left the goat here? Corey had fallen in love with this tiny creature. She couldn't bear it if he hadn't found a good home. Lots of people who adopted animals didn't know how to take care of them. What if the people who were adopting this goat didn't take care of him properly? He was still a baby. What if they let him get sick or—Corey could barely say the word to herself—*die*?

"Oh, no, Alexander, that's not going to happen to you," she said. Without realizing it, she'd just given the kid a name. "No way. I'm going to take care of you myself!"

Then, without another thought, Corey took the sleeping kid in her arms and stood up. She had to get him home and she had to do it right away. In a matter of minutes, the riding show would be over. The goat's new owner would probably be looking for him.

Corey slipped Alexander back into his cage and clipped the door shut. She tore the adoption papers off the cage and ripped them up.

She added the tiny pieces of paper to the newspaper in the bottom of Alexander's cage. She picked the cage up by its handle and hurried out of the paddock, away from Pine Hollow and away from the crowd around the arena. The only thing on her mind was that she had to get home before her father got there. Otherwise, she'd never get Alexander into her room.

5 Back Home

"Okay, Sam, it's time for you to go home," May said to Corey's pony. She and Jasmine had already unloaded Macaroni and Outlaw from the van. Now it was Sam's turn.

Whenever Corey stayed at her father's apartment, May and Jasmine took care of Sam. They loved Corey's pony almost as much as she did. They took very good care of him.

May took his lead. Jasmine patted his flank. He stepped forward and was out of the van in a flash.

"Very good!" said May.

"I think he's trying to make up for being naughty this afternoon," said Jasmine.

"I don't think that was really his fault," said May. "He can't help it. It's in his nature to get into trouble."

Jasmine laughed. "Isn't that exactly what

you told your teacher about yourself last week?'' she teased.

May nodded. "Sam and I have a lot in common,'' she said. "We both do things we don't mean to sometimes.''

She hugged him. "Don't worry, Sam. Tomorrow will be better. And we'll take good care of you until Corey gets back,'' May promised.

She took his lead rope and he followed her right into Corey's backyard, where his stable was. Corey's mother was there, waiting for them.

"I thought you'd want to know we found Corey. She's at her father's apartment. I just talked to him. She went straight there from Pine Hollow.''

"Is she still feeling bad?'' asked Jasmine.

"Her father says she's fine—though she's spending a lot of time in her room,'' Doc Tock replied. "I'm sure she'll be herself again by tomorrow.''

"Sam too,'' Jasmine added.

Doc Tock nodded. "They'll both be okay.'' A frown crossed her face. "I wish I could say the same for one of the CARL animals.''

"What's the problem?'' Jasmine asked. "I thought lots of animals got adopted today.''

"They did,'' Doc Tock said. "But a goat we

brought to the demonstration is missing. It's very strange. The owner left the goat in its cage in a paddock at Pine Hollow. When he came back to get it, the goat and the cage were gone."

"That cute little black-and-white one?" May asked.

"That's the one," said Doc Tock. "Some of our volunteers spent a long time looking for it after the show was over. There wasn't a sign of it, though." The vet sighed. "The goat is very young—it can't survive on its own. If someone took him, I hope he or she knows how to care for him."

"He's so cute!" Jasmine said. "I hope nothing happens to him."

"We can look for him some more next time we go to Pine Hollow," said May. "We'll tell our friends, too."

"Good," said Doc Tock. "That will be very helpful. Thank you. And thank you, too, for looking after Sam."

"No problem," said May.

"We're the Pony Tails," Jasmine reminded her.

"Corey is lucky to have such nice and pony-crazy friends," Doc Tock said.

It didn't take long for the girls to settle the

pony. They put a sheet on him and gave him fresh hay and water. Sam chomped on the hay happily.

Jasmine closed his stall door and watched him. Thoughtfully, she turned to May. "Maybe we should call Corey and see how she's do-ing," she suggested. "We can tell her that Sam seems much better. And we can tell her the show was a big success."

May shook her head. "Trust me, Jasmine. The worst thing would be to talk to Corey about riding and ponies. Let's just leave her alone and let her come to us."

"Okay," Jasmine agreed with a sigh.

A few minutes later she said good-bye to May and Sam. "I'll see you later," Jasmine told May. The Pony Tails often had sleepovers on Saturday nights. Tonight Jasmine was sleeping at May's.

As she led Outlaw home, Jasmine thought about Corey some more. It was so hard to stop herself from calling her. She just knew she could cheer Corey up and make her feel better about the day.

May's right, she tried to convince herself. The best thing to do is leave Corey alone.

6 Peace and Quiet

"Bleeaaa!"

"Shhh," Corey shushed Alexander.

"Corey, are you all right?" Mr. Takamura asked through Corey's bedroom door.

"Yeah, Dad, I'm really okay," she said. "I just need to be alone."

"But that sound . . . ," her father said. "Are you sure everything's okay?"

Corey tried to think. She had to say something to him. What would May do? she wondered. Then she knew what to say.

"My stomach's a little upset," she fibbed.

"That was a burp?" Mr. Takamura asked. He sounded as if he didn't quite believe it.

"I feel much better now," Corey said.

"Bleeaaaaa!"

"Corey?"

"I'm fine, Dad. I think I'll just lie down. I'd

like to take a little nap now. I just need to be by myself."

"I understand, Corey," said Mr. Takamura. "But please tell me if there's anything I can do for you."

"I will, Dad," Corey promised. Corey listened as her father's footsteps moved away from her bedroom door. He went into the living room and turned on the television set to watch the news.

Corey sighed with relief. She would have to think of some other solution soon. Her father would never let her keep Alexander if he found him. Pets weren't allowed in his apartment—not even cats or dogs. What would he say about a goat?

"Whew," Corey said. Then she turned to her bed, but she didn't lie down on it. She couldn't lie down on it. Alexander's cage was sitting on it.

"You've got to stop that bleating," she whispered. "We're going to be in big trouble!"

"Bleeaaaa!" came the goat's reply.

Corey pulled a blanket over the kid's cage to muffle the sound. That just made Alexander bleat more loudly.

She had to do something else. Again she asked herself, What would May do?

Corey in the Saddle

Of course! She stood up and went over to the small stereo set her father had given her for her last birthday. She flicked on the radio and tuned in to a hard-rock station.

There was a crash of cymbals, then the loud twang of electric guitars.

"Perfect!" Corey declared. It was just what she needed.

She turned up the volume. Her father would never be able to hear Alexander over that.

"Corey!" her father yelled. "What's going on?"

"I'm napping," she called back.

"With all that racket going on?" he asked.

"Isn't it great music?" she asked.

"Uh, sure," said Mr. Takamura.

To her surprise her father didn't ask her to turn the music down. Maybe he'd decided she'd had enough troubles for one day.

In spite of everything, Corey smiled. She'd probably managed to convince her father that her stomach was all right. Now he might be more worried about her ears—or her head!

*　　*　　*

"Come on, we just have to call her," Jasmine said. She and May were sitting on the floor of May's room in their pajamas. For three whole hours Jasmine had kept herself from calling Corey. She couldn't wait any longer. The three Pony Tails were always together.

May finally gave in. "Okay. But we can't mention ponies."

"No problem," Jasmine agreed quickly. "We're friends—we have other stuff to talk about."

"Don't bring up the demonstration, either," warned May.

"I won't," Jasmine insisted. "Come on!"

May and Jasmine hurried down the hall to the phone. May dialed the number.

Mr. Takamura answered. It was hard to hear him.

"It's May," she said loudly. "May Grover."

"What?" said Corey's father.

May put her hand over the receiver. "There's an awful racket going on there," she told Jasmine. "Mr. Takamura's neighbor must be playing rock music."

"What?" Mr. Takamura said again.

"Is Corey there? It's May. May Grover. Jasmine's here, too."

Finally Mr. Takamura got it. "Hang on a minute," he said.

The girls waited. In a few minutes May heard the noise stop. Then Corey was on the phone.

"Uh, hi," she said. She sounded very nervous.

May decided to jump in and talk about something besides ponies, riding, and drill demonstrations. That meant she had to find another subject. That was easy.

"Who was playing that awful music?" May asked. "I could barely hear your father."

"Uh, that was me. Don't you like rock?" Corey asked.

May did like rock music. But only someone who was very hard of hearing could have liked it that loud!

"Listen, May," Corey said. "I'm a little busy now. I can't talk long."

"Oh," May said, feeling a little hurt. "Uh, well, Jasmine wants to talk to you, too." She quickly handed the phone to Jasmine.

"Hi!" Jasmine said cheerfully. "What's up?"

"Like I said to May, I'm a little busy now . . . ," Corey began.

"Are you doing homework or something?" Jasmine asked.

"Just listening to some music," said Corey.

"Oh," said Jasmine. She opened her mouth to tell Corey that Sam was fine. Then she quickly closed it. She couldn't talk about Sam. She'd have to think of something else to say to Corey. But what?

Corey in the Saddle

Suddenly Corey solved the problem for her. "I'll see you at school," Corey said. "Bye."

Jasmine mumbled good-bye, then hung up. She stared at May with a miserable expression on her face. "It's worse than I thought," she said. "Corey didn't say a word about ponies. She hardly said anything at all."

"I know," May replied. "We just have to be patient, Jasmine," she reminded her friend again. "Remember how Doc Tock said Corey would be herself by tomorrow? Well, I bet Corey calls us first thing in the morning to ask about Sam."

Jasmine nodded, then followed May back to her room. How could Corey not even mention Sam? she wondered. Or bring up the demonstration?

The two girls climbed into their sleeping bags, which were rolled out on the floor of May's room. Jasmine told May about a new feed she was trying on Outlaw. May told Jasmine about braiding Macaroni's mane. They talked pony talk until Mrs. Grover knocked on the door and said, "Lights out, girls."

Jasmine told herself that tonight was just like any other Pony Tails sleepover. But there was a big difference, and she knew it.

One of the Pony Tails wasn't riding her pony anymore.

7 Back at School

By Monday morning, Corey was going crazy. She'd managed to hide Alexander from her father all day on Sunday, but it hadn't been easy. She'd barely slept a wink on Sunday night. The awful music she'd been playing gave her nightmares! And everytime she did get to sleep, Alexander started fussing in his cage and woke her. The music probably gave him nightmares, too! she thought.

Corey thought everything would be better in the morning—until she had to feed Alexander. He was very, very hungry for a *lot* of milk. She tried to sneak three glasses of it into her room for him. Alexander liked that. Corey's father didn't.

"You know I don't want you to take food into your room," he said.

"But I have to finish my homework while I

have some breakfast," Corey lied. "What was the name of the Native American tribe that greeted the Pilgrims?" she added quickly.

"Wampanoag," said Mr. Takamura.

"Thanks, Dad," Corey said. "I'll be ready in a minute." She slipped into her room, closed the door, and turned on the music.

Guitars blasted and drums banged while she fed Alexander.

"I have to go to school now," she whispered, knowing he could barely hear her over the music. It didn't matter. Even if he could hear her, he couldn't understand her. "Don't worry, though. I'll be back this afternoon."

Alexander looked at her curiously. Corey hoped he understood at least some of what she was saying.

As she gathered up her books for school, she let out a sigh. She dreaded facing her friends. It was the first time since the show that she'd have to see the Pony Tails and the other riders from Pine Hollow.

Corey still felt ashamed when she thought about the drill demonstration. May and Jasmine had called her on Saturday night and yesterday, too, but they hadn't mentioned the demonstration or Sam at all.

That's because they're embarrassed for me,

she thought. They don't want to tell me that Sam and I ruined the show.

A lump formed in Corey's throat. She missed Sam and she missed her friends.

Don't think about it, she ordered herself. She was never getting on a horse or pony again— and that was that. At least she had Alexander. Just the sight of the cute little kid made Corey feel better. She might have failed with Sam, but she knew she was doing a good job with Alexander. She'd been taking care of the baby goat on her own for two whole days.

Corey clipped a bottle into his cage. "Be good while I'm gone," she told him. He watched her every move as she got ready to leave. On her way out, she put her finger to her lips to tell Alexander to be quiet. She couldn't leave her radio playing all day.

Mr. Takamura taught at the high school next to the elementary school. He and Corey always walked to school together. As they left the apartment this morning, Alexander was quiet.

It's a miracle, Corey thought. She hoped it would last.

All morning, Corey worried about the baby goat. Had Alexander's bottle fallen out of the rack in his cage? she thought as her teacher took attendance.

And while the class talked about Plimouth Plantation, Corey was thinking, He must be so lonely.

In music, while the other children were singing "Old MacDonald," Corey was sure she could hear Alexander bleating.

At lunchtime, Corey did her best to avoid Jasmine and May. She ate lunch quickly, then went to the library instead of going outside. She still wasn't ready to talk about the demonstration—or tell them about Alexander. For now she wanted to keep the goat her secret.

But Corey couldn't avoid the Pony Tails altogether. After school Jasmine and May were waiting for her by the front steps.

Corey took a deep breath.

"We're going to the shopping center," Jasmine began. "Want to—"

"No, I can't," interrupted Corey. "I've got to get home right away."

"Maybe we could come with you?" May asked.

Corey panicked. "Uh, I have a lot of homework," she said quickly.

"We could help," Jasmine offered.

"No thanks. I've got to do it by myself," said Corey.

For a few minutes there was silence. May

Corey in the Saddle

was getting desperate. Finally she thought of something to say.

"Hey, Corey, did your mother tell you about the goat?"

"Goat? What goat?" Corey's eyes went wide.

"The one from CARL," said May. "He's missing."

Corey could feel her heart start racing. "It must have run away," she said. "Sometimes baby animals run away because they're scared."

"I don't think so." Jasmine shook her head.

"Why not?" Corey asked.

"Because its cage was gone, too," May explained. "Your mom thinks someone kidnapped him."

Corey gulped. "Oh," she said. "Well, I don't know anything about it."

"It's very serious," May went on. "The people from CARL are worried about him. He's very young and can't survive on his own. He needs someone to take care of him or he'll die."

Jasmine nodded. "Who would steal a baby goat?" she said. "It seems almost cruel."

"Alexander's fine," Corey blurted out. "He . . ." As soon as the words left her lips, she knew she'd made a mistake.

Pony Tails

"Who's Alexander?" Jasmine looked puzzled.

Corey felt herself blush. "That's the goat's name. I mean, that's what I would call him if he belonged to me."

"Oh," said May.

Jasmine still looked a little confused.

"I've got to go," Corey said before May or Jasmine could ask any more questions. "See you."

A second later Corey was gone.

The two remaining Pony Tails looked at each other.

Jasmine gulped. "Uh-oh," she said. "Corey still didn't ask about Sam."

"I know," May said. "I don't know what to do. I thought for sure Corey would have mentioned Sam by now."

It was Jasmine's turn to try to reassure May. "Corey can't ignore him forever," she pointed out. "Wednesday is our riding lesson at Pine Hollow. It's also Corey's day to come home to her mom's. Sam will be right there in her own backyard. She'll have to ride then."

"But what if—" May began.

Jasmine interrupted her. "May, you have to be more patient!" she said.

May laughed as she heard her own words

coming back at her. "You're right, Jasmine. Thanks," she said.

"You're welcome," Jasmine answered. "That's what the Pony Tails are here for—to help each other."

Now May felt much better. Jasmine was right. The Pony Tails knew how to help each other. Together they would get Corey back in the saddle—even if it took a little longer than they expected!

8 Pony Tails at Home

On Wednesday afternoon, Jasmine peered out the window of May's room. She'd been watching Corey's backyard since she and May had gotten home from Pine Hollow.

"Don't worry, Jasmine," May called. "Corey will go straight to the stable to see Sam when she gets home."

"I know," Jasmine replied. "Of course that's what she'll do."

Jasmine and May sounded cheerful. But inside they were getting more and more worried. Corey hadn't been at riding class that afternoon. Instead she'd dashed out of school, mumbling something about having to hurry to her father's apartment.

What if she really never rides again? thought Jasmine. What would happen to the Pony

Corey in the Saddle

Tails? And poor Sam. He . . . Suddenly Jasmine saw something. "Hey, wait a minute, May!" she cried. "The back door is opening. . . ."

May hopped up from her bed and went to watch with Jasmine.

There was Corey. She was struggling to carry an enormous box wrapped in a blanket. Nervously she glanced around her backyard.

"What is she doing?" May asked.

"Beats me," replied Jasmine. She kept her eyes fixed on her friend. "Maybe it's a surprise for Samurai."

"Maybe," May echoed. "I hope so."

Corey disappeared into the stable.

"Should we go see her and help her groom Sam?" Jasmine asked.

May shook her head. "Let's just let her spend some time alone with Sam. Once she sees him, she's going to want to ride him—I'm sure of it."

Jasmine nodded. That sounded right to her. Now all they had to do was keep on waiting. That was getting harder and harder to do.

"Maybe we can play Crazy Eights or something," Jasmine said.

"Good idea," May said. She reached into a drawer for a deck of cards.

Pony Tails

Next door, Corey hurried into the dark stable.

"Hush now, Alexander," she whispered to the heavy load in her arms. "You're almost at your new home. And when you're here, you won't have to listen to awful music."

The thought made Corey smile. Keeping the kid at her father's had been nearly impossible. Luckily, the music had helped her hide him. But now Corey didn't care if she ever heard rock and roll again!

Corey was glad she'd finally gotten the goat here. Alexander was a tiny baby, but his cage was very heavy. She didn't know what she'd do when it was time to go back to her father's apartment. She was still trying to figure out how to deal with him at her mother's.

She was also trying to think of a way to keep her secret from her friends. So far it had been pretty easy. The other Pony Tails weren't exactly ignoring her. But they hadn't said a word about riding or asked her why she hadn't come to Pony Club.

Now that she was next door again, things would be a little more tricky.

As Corey lugged the heavy cage through the stable, a sound suddenly broke the quiet.

"Whhhnnnnn!"

Corey in the Saddle

Corey swallowed. It was Sam, welcoming her home.

In front of Sam's stall, Corey put down Alexander's cage. She took off the blanket that covered the cage.

"Bleeaaaaa!"

"Whhhnnnnn!" a startled Sam said.

"Bleeaaa!" Alexander replied.

Corey looked back and forth, from goat to pony, as the two animals continued making sounds.

Every time the pony whinnied, the baby goat bleated.

"Are you two talking to one another?" Corey asked in amazement.

They were. Alexander and Sam chattered back and forth like old friends!

Corey grinned and shook her head. Working with her mother had taught her that animals often do surprising things. By now she was convinced that they shared as many secrets with each other as humans did between themselves!

There was a small space in the stable where Corey planned to keep Alexander. Sam was Corey's responsibility, so Doc Tock rarely came out there. Corey was hoping that Alexander's noises wouldn't be noticed among all the other animal sounds around the house.

Corey in the Saddle

Corey put fresh straw and water in the little coop next to Sam's stall. She ran inside the house to get fresh milk for Alexander. She filled his bottle and clipped it to the side of the coop, and then she was ready.

Sam watched carefully as Corey let Alexander out of the cage. She led Alexander over to the coop.

The goat sniffed every inch of the space. Then he pranced around it. In another two minutes, he was happily tugging at his bottle.

"He likes his new home!" Corey exclaimed. Then she knew she had one more important thing to do.

Corey turned to face Sam. It had been four whole days since she'd seen him. And she'd been so busy with Alexander, she hadn't even let herself think about her pony.

Sam had water and hay. His feed bucket had been filled that morning. Her friends had done a good job of taking care of him. It was just like they always did, Corey thought.

Sam sniffed Corey's shirt pockets, hoping to find a carrot or an apple. But she'd been so busy with Alexander, she hadn't even thought to bring her pony a present!

Suddenly tears spilled down Corey's cheeks. Sam reached his soft nose forward and nuzzled Corey's cheek. Corey reached up and hugged him, pressing her face against his.

"Oh, Sam, I'm so sorry," she whispered. "I was mad at you on Saturday, but it was my fault, too! I was too nervous to ride well."

The pony blinked at her. "Don't worry," Corey told him. "It won't happen again. I've decided to take a break from riding."

Sam gently nudged her with his nose. He was asking Corey to pet him.

Corey patted Sam's neck and rubbed his face where he liked it best. He stepped closer to her, enjoying the attention.

Corey knew her pony was glad that she was home. And now that she wasn't mad anymore, she was happy to be here with him.

Even if she wouldn't be riding him for a long, long time.

9 The Truth Comes Out

Corey spent the next few days taking care of Alexander. She also made sure to spend extra time with Sam. After ignoring him for four days, she had a lot to make up to her pony.

She brought Sam an apple after school on Friday. "Here you go, boy." She patted his nose, then watched him gobble up the crunchy treat.

Corey knew the extra attention was helping her pony. But she also knew that Sam needed a rider. Ponies—especially young, frisky ponies like Sam—needed exercise.

"Maybe we can ask May and Jasmine to ride you this weekend," she said.

Thinking about her friends made Corey sigh. Six days had passed since the show at Pine Hollow. And during that time, the

Pony Tails

Pony Tails hadn't talked about ponies or riding at all. Nothing like this had ever happened before.

One part of Corey was relieved. She didn't want to talk about the show or her performance. But another part was worried. Jasmine and May were her best friends. The three of them were the Pony Tails.

If Corey wasn't riding with them, or talking about ponies with them, what would happen to their friendship?

Just then Sam snorted loudly.

"Bleeaaa!" Alexander chimed in.

Corey laughed. Her pony was saying that he wanted another apple. And Alexander seemed to be telling her to give it to him.

She gave Sam a big hug instead. "I'll be back tomorrow with another treat for you," she said. Then she stood up and said good-bye to her pony and the baby goat. She felt a little sad leaving them. But she knew they would keep each other company.

*   *   *

The next morning Corey grabbed a carton of milk and hurried to the stable. She had gotten up extra early, to take care of her pets and to do something else: figure out what to do about Alexander. This afternoon she was supposed to go back to her father's. How was she going to take the goat with her?

"Whnnnhhhhh!" Sam greeted her when she opened the door.

"Good morning, Sam," she said. Then she listened for Alexander's bleat from his coop. But it didn't come. Sam whinnied again.

Silence.

Corey hurried to Alexander's coop. She peered in. She couldn't see anything. She turned on the light and looked again. She still couldn't see anything.

Then she did see something. It was the door to the coop. It was wide open. The coop was empty. Alexander was gone!

A horrible knot squeezed Corey's stomach. It was a familiar feeling. Sam had run away once, too. He had eventually come back on his own, but it was awful while he was gone. And now Alexander had disappeared.

Corey's mind raced. Sam had long legs. He'd been able to go so far that Corey and her friends couldn't find him. Alexander was a tiny baby with short legs. How far could he go?

Corey stepped out of the stable.

"Alexander!" she called. There was no answer. "Alexander!" Nothing.

She looked around at the three backyards— hers, May's and Jasmine's. She couldn't see any sign of him there, or in the fields beyond the girls' houses. What she did see, though, was May. May was going from her house to the stable to look after Macaroni.

May waved at Corey. Corey waved back.

"What's up?" May called.

Tears filled Corey's eyes. What had she been thinking? Why had she taken the baby goat and hidden him from her friends and family? What a crazy idea! If something had happened to him, she'd never forgive herself.

Corey knew then that she couldn't keep her secret any longer. She had to tell her friends about Alexander. She ran over to May's yard.

"What's the matter?" May asked.

"Alexander's missing," said Corey.

"Oh, that goat? Sure, I told you about that, remember?" May asked.

"No, I mean *really* missing," said Corey.

May looked at Corey oddly. Her friend had been acting very strange lately. Maybe not riding Samurai was affecting her brain!

"He's been missing since Saturday," May said patiently. She sounded as if she were explaining it to a little child. "Somebody took him from Pine Hollow."

"You don't understand, May," Corey said. "*I'm* the one who took him from Pine Hollow."

"Don't be silly," said May. "How could you

keep a . . ." Then the light came on. "Oh, the music . . ."

Corey nodded.

"And sneaking into your stable . . ." said May.

Corey nodded.

"And dashing home after school . . ." said May. She started to ask Corey why she'd taken the goat. She stopped herself when she saw her friend's tears. Right now that wasn't important.

"Now he's gone," Corey said. "He disappeared overnight."

"Then we have to find him," said May. "He must have run into the fields." She didn't want to say it, but a little goat could have a lot of fun—and get into a lot of trouble—out there.

"Let's get Jasmine," she said instead. "And our ponies. We can do this a lot faster if we don't do it on foot."

At that moment Jasmine came out of her house. As she headed toward Outlaw's stable, she saw her two friends at May's house. She ran over to join them.

It took only a minute to explain to Jasmine what had happened.

"Well, then why don't we use our ponies to see if we can find Alexander in the field?" Jasmine asked.

"That's what May said," Corey said slowly. The two other Pony Tails watched her face carefully.

"Are you ready to ride?" May asked gently.

Corey took a deep breath. Suddenly staying out of the saddle seemed silly. Especially at a time like this. Of course you're ready to ride, she told herself. You're one of the Pony Tails.

She nodded at her friends.

"Then let's tack up," said Jasmine. "Meet you guys in ten minutes!"

"Make it eight!" said May.

"I'll make it *five*," Corey promised.

Then May, Jasmine, and Corey each said exactly the same thing at exactly the same time:

"The Pony Tails are back in the saddle!"

The three girls took only a second to look at one another and grin. Then they did exactly what they always did when they said the same thing at the same time. They reached up and slapped hands together.

"Jake!" they cried.

Five minutes later they met in May's paddock.

The Pony Tails were ready to ride.

10 Looking for Alexander

As the Pony Tails left the paddock behind the Grovers' house, Corey could feel Sam eagerly prancing. He was ready to go and alert to everything she told him. When she touched his belly with her heels, he moved forward in a walk. Just a little more pressure from her brought a trot.

Corey found herself thinking about their performance last week at Pine Hollow. Rider and pony were much more together this time!

"Let's go, boy!" she urged Sam. "We've got to find Alexander!" At the mention of his friend's name, Sam's ears flicked back.

"Here's how we'll do it," May said. "I'll check near the woods. I don't think Alexander could have gotten that far, but I'll look for tracks. Jasmine, you take the right half of the field. Corey, you go to the left."

Corey grinned. Things were back to normal. May was taking charge, as usual. Suddenly she had no doubt they'd find the goat.

"We should all look for signs that he's been around," said Jasmine.

"Right," Corey agreed. "Alexander isn't very big, but he might have left a path through the grass. He might even have stopped to eat some grass, though so far all he's had is milk. He also bleats loudly, so listen for that, too."

May headed to the left to make a circle around the field. She never took her eyes off the ground around her. She saw a lot of things: mole holes in the ground, an old bird's nest, a withered bunch of wildflowers, even the strap from her riding helmet, which she'd lost last spring. What she didn't see was Alexander or any sign of him at all.

Jasmine followed May's instructions. She went back and forth across the field, making a path like a lawn mower. Outlaw walked slowly while she looked around.

"Here, Alexander!" she called out from time to time. Then she waited and listened for a bleat in response. All she heard, though, was Corey calling him, too.

Jasmine decided to try to bleat instead.

Corey in the Saddle

Maybe the goat would answer a sound like that.

"*Blaaaaaah,*" she said.

"Did you hear that?" Corey called out. "It sounded a little like Alexander, only *very* sick!"

"It was just me," Jasmine called back, blushing. That was the end of that. She went back to calling, "Here, Alexander!" It didn't work any better, but it didn't worry Corey, either.

Corey leaned forward in the saddle. "We've just got to find him!" she said to Sam. Like Jasmine, she rode back and forth in the field. She looked closely at the ground. She called for the little kid. She listened for a response. Nothing.

The field stretched far back behind the girls' houses. Corey and her friends checked every inch of the land.

As time wore on, Corey could feel her hopes fading. Maybe the Pony Tails wouldn't find him. Alexander was so tiny—what if something terrible had happened? She forced herself to concentrate on the search. Thinking scary thoughts wouldn't help anyone.

After forty-five minutes, the girls met back at the Grovers' ring.

No one had found a trace of Alexander.

"What do we do next?" Jasmine asked. She and Corey looked at May.

But May shrugged. "I'm out of ideas. I thought he'd be in the field," she mumbled.

"Me too," said Jasmine.

Corey didn't say anything. She was wondering if it was time to get her mother's help. It was time to tell her the truth about Alexander anyway. Maybe Doc Tock would have an idea about where to find him.

For a few minutes the girls sat on their ponies, each lost in her thoughts. Macaroni stood still. That wasn't surprising. He usually did. Outlaw fussed a little. That wasn't surprising, either. He always fussed a little. Sam pulled at his reins. That wasn't surprising, either.

"Calm down, boy," Corey said. Sam stepped backward. Corey pulled a little on the reins to stop him. That made him step backward more. That made Corey grip him with her legs and tug more firmly on the reins. "Not again," Corey moaned. "We've been doing so well today."

"Sam!" Jasmine scolded her friend's pony. "This is no time to misbehave!"

Suddenly Corey had an idea. "I'm not sure he's misbehaving," she said.

"He sure is!" May said. "He's not doing anything you tell him."

"Maybe he's doing exactly what I told him to do," Corey went on.

Corey in the Saddle

"What are you talking about?" May asked.

"I'm not sure," said Corey. "But I want to try something."

Corey relaxed her hold on the reins. She stopped gripping Sam's belly with her legs. "Find Alexander!" she said.

Sam lifted his head and sniffed the air. His ears flicked around alertly. He looked to the left. Then he looked to the right. Then he began to move.

At first, Corey's pony was just walking. May and Jasmine followed Corey and Sam on their ponies. Then Sam began trotting. He turned a little bit to the right. And then he turned to the left. His ears pricked up. His nostrils flared. He shook his head excitedly. And then he began to canter.

"He's going to find him!" Jasmine cried. "He knows where Alexander is!"

Corey turned around in the saddle. She gave her friends a thumbs-up sign. Jasmine was right. Sam was following the little goat's trail.

Sam slowed down near a small pile of rocks at the edge of the field. Corey and Sam had passed these rocks before, and Corey hadn't seen anything. She still didn't see anything, but that didn't mean there wasn't anything there.

"*Whhhnnnnn!*" said Sam.

Pony Tails

"Bleeaaaa!" came a faint reply.

"Alexander!" Corey shouted triumphantly. She halted Sam, then quickly slipped down out of her saddle. She ran to where the sound had come from. And there was Alexander.

The kid had gotten himself stuck between two rocks. He was a little baby, but he wasn't as little as he'd thought. He was caught tightly and couldn't get out.

It was a hard job for a little kid, but an easy one for three Pony Tails. In just a few minutes, the girls had freed Alexander. Corey held him gently in her arms and hugged him. Jasmine and May patted him. Alexander bleated loudly.

"What does that mean?" May asked.

"It means he's hungry," said Corey.

"It's the sound he always makes, isn't it?" Jasmine asked.

"It's because he's always hungry," Corey explained.

"Bleeaaaaa!" said Alexander.

Corey climbed into her saddle and May handed the kid up to her. The three girls turned their ponies around to head back to their stables.

Doc Tock was waiting for Corey when they got home. Her eyes went wide when she saw Corey on Sam. They opened wider when she saw the bundle in Corey's arms.

"Uh, Mom, I can . . . explain," Corey said doubtfully. "It's a long story."

"That's the goat that got kidnapped," Doc Tock said. "And you found him."

"Actually, I was the one who kidnapped him," Corey said. "Sam is the one who found him."

First Doc Tock looked startled. Then she looked angry. But all she said was, "Let me check my patient. Then you and I will talk, Corey."

Corey handed Alexander over to her mother. "Okay," she said softly.

Doc Tock took Alexander to her clinic inside the house.

"Are you in trouble?" Jasmine whispered.

"I think so," Corey replied. "What I did was really stupid. Alexander could have died because of me. And one thing my mom won't put up with is careless treatment of animals."

May and Jasmine hugged Corey. "We'll put Macaroni and Outlaw away and wait for you at your stable," Jasmine said.

Corey thanked her friends for all their help, then she led Sam home.

"Good boy," she told him. "You're a hero. I'm so sorry for the way I treated you *and* Alexander."

Corey in the Saddle

Corey untacked her pony and gave him some water. She made sure his stall was clean and comfortable. After she'd done everything she could for Sam, she took a deep breath.

It was time to go in and face her mother.

11 Best Friends

"Well?" Jasmine demanded when Corey entered the stable an hour later. She was carrying Alexander. "What happened?"

"Are you grounded for life?" May asked nervously. She thought that would be her punishment if she'd kidnapped a goat.

Corey hung her head. "Believe it or not . . . ," she began sadly. "I have to do ten hours of volunteer work at CARL!" When she looked up, her face was shining.

"Ten hours of work at CARL!" May echoed. "That's not a punishment—it's fun!"

"I know," Corey agreed. She took Alexander over to his coop and placed him inside. Jasmine helped her clip a fresh bottle of milk into the holder.

The girls watched Alexander tug at the nipple. "He's really cute!" Jasmine sighed. "No wonder you took him, Corey."

From his stall next door, Sam watched everything like an attentive mother.

"You're cute, too," Corey told her pony. She went over to pat him. "My mother called my father while I was there. They talked about it and decided the work at CARL would be fair. I think Dad was so relieved he wasn't going to have to listen to any more rock, he wanted to let me off scot-free."

May laughed. "I'm with him!"

"But what's going to happen to Alexander?" Jasmine asked. The goat had finished his bottle and was curled up, ready to go to sleep. "Is the person who adopted him going to get him?"

"Mom called him, too, to say that Alexander was safe." Corey laughed. "But as soon as he heard the name Alexander, he changed his mind about adopting him. He wanted a female goat!"

"So, what's going to happen to Alexander?" Jasmine repeated her question. "Are you going to adopt him?"

"Not me," Corey said. "I've thought really hard. Alexander needs someone who can be with him all the time, someone who can be his best friend, who will keep him company and look after him if he decides to run away again."

"So you have to give him up?" May asked.

"Not exactly," said Corey. "Mom and I think the perfect home for Alexander is our stable."

"I thought you weren't going to adopt him," said May. She was confused.

"Not *me*," said Corey. "Sam. Sam is a perfect best friend for Alexander. And Alexander seems to have helped him calm down, too."

"Great!" said May.

"Whnnnhhhhh!" said Sam.

"Bleeeaaaaa!" Alexander bleated softly. By now he was half-asleep.

"The only problem is that the two of them chatter back and forth all the time," Corey went on. "I'll never be able to hear myself think in here!"

May and Jasmine laughed.

"I wonder what they talk about," Jasmine said.

Corey shrugged. "Whatever best friends usually talk about."

For a few minutes, an uncomfortable silence fell between the girls. They were each thinking about how the three of them hadn't been talking much at all.

Then May spoke up. "Well, my plan worked," she said.

Corey in the Saddle

"Stop bragging." Jasmine grinned.

"What are you talking about?" Corey asked. "What plan?"

"My plan to get you back in the saddle," May answered proudly.

"May said if we tried to push you into riding, it wouldn't work. We had to wait until you were ready," Jasmine explained. "I wasn't sure, but as usual I went along with her. Boy, was it hard *not* to talk about ponies with you!"

Corey stared at her friends, amazed. "Do you know what I thought?" she said. "I thought you didn't want to talk about ponies because I'm a terrible rider. I thought you guys agreed I shouldn't ride anymore."

Jasmine laughed. "Corey! How could you think a thing like that?"

"Easy," Corey answered. "Sam and I were terrible at the drill demonstration."

"At Pony Club I was telling Lisa Atwood about you and Sam," Jasmine began. "She told me that she had a friend named Kate who stopped riding for a while, too."

Corey remembered how Lisa had tried to give her some advice on the day of the drill. The older rider had seemed to know exactly how Corey felt. "Did Kate ever get back in the saddle?" asked Corey.

Jasmine nodded. "Eventually she decided

she loved to ride, but she didn't like to compete. It's too much pressure."

"I know that feeling," Corey said. "I was so nervous that day. I have to learn how to handle shows better."

"That's true," agreed May. "But Max says that horses and riders just have bad days sometimes. Maybe that's what happened to you and Sam."

Corey nodded. "I've done some dumb things this week. But I've learned a lot, too."

"Oh really, Ms. Takamura," May said. Jasmine and Corey laughed as she imitated her teacher's high-pitched voice. "And would you like to tell the class what you've learned?"

"Yes, teacher," Corey answered. "One thing is to be more patient with my pony. I also have to be more patient with his rider."

"Very good," May said. "Go on, please."

"Another thing"—Corey smiled at her friends—"is that I love being part of the Pony Tails."

"And we love having you," Jasmine said quickly.

"And last, but not least, my mom reminded me to put animals first," Corey said.

"Does that mean it was wrong to kidnap the kid?" Jasmine's eyes were twinkling.

Pony Tails

"Exactly," Corey said, and at that the three of them burst out laughing.

As the merry sound filled the stable, Alexander woke up and opened his eyes.

"Bleeeaaa," said the kid.

"Whnnnhhh," Sam added from his stall.

Corey smiled happily. The two best friends were sharing secrets again—and so were the Pony Tails!

COREY'S TIPS
FOR A HEALTHY PONY

Everybody knows that my mother is a vet. In her practice, she takes care of small animals, but she always says that anybody who owns an animal has to be part vet. That means that the owner is the most important person when it comes to the pet's health.

The first thing a pony owner has to do is keep good records. At Horse Wise, our Pony Club, Max gives us forms for recording information. An owner can also keep a notebook for each horse or pony, or make up sheets for herself. The medical record should show when horses have problems and what treatment they get. They also need to show when the animal gets shots and gets wormed.

Pony Tails

Also, every owner should keep records of a pony when he's healthy. That way the vet will have something to compare it to when the pony gets sick.

For example, most ponies and horses have a normal temperature of about 100 degrees when they are healthy. If a pony's temperature goes over 101 degrees, the owner should call the vet. Sam's normal temperature is closer to 99.5 degrees, so when his goes over 100.5 degrees, I call the vet.

Two other things an owner has to watch are a pony's pulse and respiration rate. That means how often his heart beats in a minute and how many times he takes a breath in a minute. You take a pony's pulse by feeling under his chin by his jawbone. His pulse should be about forty-five beats a minute. If he's just been exercising, it could be twice that and still be normal. But if he hasn't been exercising and he's got a fast pulse, it could mean he's got a fever.

You can count the number of breaths a pony takes by watching his belly. A normal, relaxed pony breathes about twelve times a minute. If your pony is at rest and is panting, you'll need to get some help.

Mom is a real stickler for getting pets immu-

Tips for a Healthy Pony

nized. She checks to make sure my records on shots are completely up to date. Horses can get a lot of diseases if they don't get their shots on time. All horses and ponies have to be immunized against diseases like tetanus and distemper. You and your vet can talk about the schedule for these, as well as other vaccinations your pony needs.

I don't like getting shots and neither does Sam! I always make sure to give him a lump of sugar, which cheers him up fast.

Another thing pony owners have to look out for is—Yuck!—parasites. Parasites such as worms live inside ponies, and others, such as fleas and ticks, live outside them on their coats. Ponies have to get preventive treatment for both kinds. Whenever the Pony Tails see ticks or fleas on our ponies, we get rid of them right away. They can make a pony very uncomfortable (as well as sick). An uncomfortable pony will find a way to make his rider uncomfortable, too!

The most important thing for an owner, Mom says, is to know what's normal about the pony. If he's usually well-behaved and then one day he's fussy, it may be a sign that he's coming down with something. Ponies, like people, have different moods (and boy, is that ever true of my pony!). When their moods are different from what their usual moods are, you'll need to keep an eye on them.

Here are some danger signs to look for: swelling (anywhere on the pony), especially if the area is also warm; loss of appetite; bare spots on his coat; coughing; runny nose or eyes; general listlessness; and cuts or sores.

Now that I own a goat as well as a pony, I'm going to have to learn a whole new branch of veterinary medicine. First I'll have to learn everything I can about what's normal for Alexander. Then I'll know if he gets sick.

A healthy pony is a happy pony, and a happy pony has a happy rider. So don't forget my mother's motto: When in doubt, call the vet!

About the Author

Bonnie Bryant was born and raised in New York City, and she still lives there today. She spends her summers in a house on a lake in Massachusetts.

Ms. Bryant began writing about girls and horses when she started The Saddle Club in 1987. So far there are more than sixty books in that series. Much as she likes telling the stories about Stevie, Carole, and Lisa, she decided that the younger riders at Pine Hollow Stables, especially May Grover, have stories of their own that need telling. That's how Pony Tails was born.

Ms. Bryant rides horses when she has time away from her computer, but she doesn't have a horse of her own. She likes to ride different horses and enjoys a variety of riding experiences. She says she thinks most of her readers are much better riders than she is!